Malcolm has had a very successful working life as a QHSE consultant and management systems auditor, mainly within the oil and gas sector. When not working as a consultant, or writing, Malcolm plays golf and was Captain of Letham Grange Golf Club for five years, he plays guitar in a part time band 'Nameless' and has written over sixty songs and produced two CDs which he hopes to sell in aid of Parkinson's.

To my wife, Dorothy, who encouraged me to finally write down the stories I told to all our nephews and nieces over the years and for correcting all my grammatical errors. To my young neighbour Nia who read my first draft of this book and whose enthusiasm gave me such encouragement to finish it.

MJM Turner

PACEY AND THE SECRETS OF THE WATER TOWER

AUSTIN MACAULEY PUBLISHERS™

LONDON • CAMBRIDGE • NEW YORK • SHARJAH

A CIP catalogue record for this title is available from the British Library.

ISBN 9781398431829 (Paperback)
ISBN 9781398431836 (ePub e-book)

www.austinmacauley.com

First Published 2023
Austin Macauley Publishers Ltd®
1 Canada Square
Canary Wharf
London
E14 5AA

Table of Contents

Chapter I
Arrival

"Right, you three, up the stairs and unpack your cases," said Great Aunty Dot, "dinner will be in twenty minutes, oh and mind and wash your hands."

A rumble of feet went thundering up the stairs.

"Righto," chimed three little voices from the top of the landing.

The voices belonged to Paccy, Solomon and Seth who were visiting their great aunt and uncle for a late Autumn break whilst their parents were going for a working holiday in America. This was a bit of an adventure for the trio as they had not been away from their mum and dad for more than a night. This was also the first time they had stayed with their father's aunt and uncle at Arbroath in Scotland. It had been quite a long journey to get to Arbroath, as they lived in a small town by the name of 'Tewkesbury' in England.

They should have been exhausted by the trip; instead, six lots of feet tumbled down the stairs. "Raaaaaayyyyyyy," Seth screamed, all excited.

"Now, now, you three, settle down, your great aunt will think you have been dragged up instead of brought up," said

Neil, their father, shaking his head. "You will be good for Aunty Dot and Uncle Malc, won't you?"

"Honestly, they will settle down once they get used to the place, it's all a big adventure for them," said Neil.

"Oh, I know how to deal with naughty girls and boys," replied Aunty Dot, "Don't you worry. You of all people should remember."

"Oh, I do indeed." The father laughed.

"I think she does," whispered Solomon to Pacey under his breath as his eyes melted into the carpet.

"Uh, hu," replied Pacey.

"Yes, I seem to remember your ways." Their father, who had stayed with his Aunty Dot and Uncle Malc many a time when he was young, giggled. "You will leave them in one piece though, won't you?" he said with a wicked grin all over his face.

Aunty Dot just raised her eyebrows and smiled in return.

A shiver went through three young bodies.

Aunty Dot and the three children waved goodbye to their father and then went into the dining room to have their dinner.

"Can we have our dinner watching television?" asked Pacey. "We always watch TV at this time of night, Mummy always lets us."

"Absolutely not," bellowed Aunty Dot, "do you think I came up the river Tay in a banana boat? I spoke with your parents before you came here, and I know what you are allowed and what you are not, now sit down at the table and eat your dinner. I've made a special dish of Stovies for you and after that, if you eat it all up, we'll see what kind of special pudding we can come up with for you."

"What's Stovies?" cried three little voices.

"Just try them," replied their great aunt, "Your father always loved them and I'm sure you will too, now eat."

The three heads looked at their plates in front of them and at the pile of steaming, brown-looking potatoes which had to be said, did not look all that appetising.

"Eat," thundered Aunty Dot in a voice that indicated there was no debate about to happen. "Add some brown sauce if you like and there are beans and corned beef there as well."

The reality of the adventure was beginning to hit home. However, fifteen minutes later there was not a drop of Stovies to be seen.

"They were brilliant," said Pacey, "what was in them? we have never had Stovies before."

"Oh, just some sheep's heads, a touch of pigs bladder mixed with potatoes, onions and pigs' blood." Aunty Dot laughed.

Six eyes and three mouths opened wider than was healthy.

"Don't worry," said their great aunt, still laughing, "I'm only kidding, it's just a simple dish of potatoes, onions, corned beef, sausages, some gravy and a little bit of Aunty magic." The six eyes and three mouths closed in a distinct sign of relief.

After a wonderful pudding of steamed ginger and toffee sponge and ice cream, the three were sent up to their bedrooms to get ready for bed. Pacey was in one bedroom and the two boys were sharing another.

"I'm sure you are all tired as you have had such a long journey today. Your Great Uncle Malc will be in shortly from his work and he will come up and see you when you are in bed. If you are good, he might read you a story. Mind you, if he starts to talk about ghosts in the cupboards, don't listen to him; he likes to wind children like you up. Tomorrow we will go exploring the area and let you see around the place." And with that, Aunty Dot went to clear up the dishes in the kitchen.

Half an hour later, there was a knock at the bedroom doors and in came Great Uncle Malc.

"Hellooo, kids," boomed Great Uncle Malc all cheerily, "You must be Pacey…and…you must be Solomon and that head under the blanket must be Seth?"

"No, I'm Solomon," came a voice from under the blanket.

"I knew that, ha, ha, ha." Great Uncle Malc laughed. "I just wanted to see if you did."

The two brothers looked at each other and shrugged.

"It's going to be a long three weeks," whispered Seth to his brother.

"Your Great Aunty tells me you might want a story before going to sleep, so I thought you'd want to know about the ghosts that live in the bedroom cupboards," continued the Great Uncle pretending not to hear Seth.

"Well, once upon…"

But before he could finish his sentence, there was a loud "MALCOLM, WHAT DID I TELL YOU?" bellowed from downstairs.

"Ah yes, well, maybe another day," said Great Uncle Malc a little embarrassed, "perhaps you would like to hear The Hobbit, that was a great favourite of mine when I was your age."

"What's a Hobbit?" came back three voices.

"Well, a Hobbit is a little dwarfish character that lives in a hole in the ground, not a smelly hole but a well-furnished, comfortable hole and he goes on a great adventure with a wizard called Gandalf and he fights a dragon called Smaug," replied Great Uncle Malc.

"Yeah, that sounds better," said Pacey.

"Right then, I'll read a chapter to you each night and by the time the story is finished, you'll be going home."

The three visitors listened in the dark as their Great Uncle started to read out the first chapter of the story of the Hobbit, Bilbo Baggins and his adventure with the magic ring and the dragon.

The next day, Great Uncle Malc was already away on business and Aunty Dot was preparing breakfast by the time the three adventurers came down the stairs.

Their great uncle and aunty's house was quite a large affair and there were lots of corridors leading off from each other. The trio were already eyeing up how they could have fun exploring all the nooks and crannies in the house.

"Great Aunty Dot," piped up Pacey.

"Yes," replied great Aunty Dot warily.

"Why are you Great Aunty Dot and not just 'Aunty Dot'?" inquired Pacey.

"Well," answered Great Aunty Dot, "I'm your father's Aunty and as you are his children that makes me great Aunty to you, it's just a way of describing our relationship, it doesn't mean that I am actually GREAT, unfortunately."

"Aaaaahh," said Pacey, not quite sure if she understood or not.

Before she could go on, her great Aunty said, "I can see that 'Great Aunty' and 'Great Uncle' is a bit of a mouthful, so for this holiday, let's shorten it to just 'Aunt' and 'Uncle', OK? Right, have your breakfast, get washed and dressed and we'll go out exploring."

Chapter II
The Water Tower

Pacey and her two brothers came down the stairs washed, (well sort of), dressed and ready to go investigating their new surroundings.

"OK," said Great Aunty Dot, "let's go. First, we'll take a tour of the gardens and then we will go across towards the boat pond."

At the mention of a boat pond, Solomon's eyes grew big.

The gardens were just coming to their best with all the flowers beginning to blossom. As soon as the two boys reached the garden, they went running around like two mad March Hares.

"Raaaaaayyyyyyyyyyyyy," went Seth with his arms out, pretending to be an aeroplane. "Taka, taka, taka, taka, taka," went Solomon trying to shoot his brother out the sky in his pretend Spitfire.

The trio were soon to find out there was loads of hidey-holes to play and lose themselves in during the next few weeks.

Great Aunty Dot came out of the house and shouted to the two aeroplanes (and Pacey who was wandering about the garden), "come on, you three, I have brought you some bread to feed the swans and ducks at the pond."

At the mention of ducks and swans, Pacey and the two planes came running.

"Now take my hands as we cross the road, it's very busy with cars and I don't want any accidents," said Great Aunty Dot.

"I'll shoot them down in my Spitfire." Solomon laughed.

"Oih, behave and listen to me, or we'll go back inside," said Great Aunty Dot, giving him one of her stares.

Solomon immediately knew what his father meant about her ways of controlling boys and girls and was in no doubt as to what that stare meant.

Once across the road and down the path towards the pond, they were met by a host of ducks, swans and seabirds, all vying for their attention and the bread that was in their hands.

Great Aunty Dot gave them a slice of bread each and they started to feed the birds.

"What was this pond for, Aunty Dot?" inquired Pacey.

"Well, at one time, not so long ago, it used to be where boys and girls could use up their energy by rowing around the island in the middle of the pond, which was great fun," replied her great aunt.

"But why aren't there any boats on the pond now, so that we can't go on them?" said Pacey quite indignantly.

"Well, you will have to ask the council that; I'm afraid it seems that they were scared of health and safety issues and that someone would get drowned," answered Great Aunty Dot tiredly.

"Have any boys and girls been drowned then?" asked Pacey, somewhat strangely excited.

"None that I know of, either in my time or before it," said Great Aunty Dot.

"Well, that's just daft and totally, totally unfair," went Pacey with a petted lip.

"Mmmm, quite," was the only reply from her great aunt.

As they walked around the pond, Pacey looked up and saw a huge imposing building at the top of the pond's hill.

"Woah," she cried, "what's that, Aunty Dot?"

"That's the water tower. At one time, that was where the people of Arbroath got their fresh water. It's over a hundred years old now," replied Great Aunty Dot, "of course, it's no longer in use these days as Arbroath is far too big for the size of the tower. All the water now comes from a local dam. It is now just a rather nice landmark and a reminder of how we used to build beautiful buildings even for mundane things."

"Can we go explore it, please, please, please, Aunty Dot?" said the excited Solomon.

"Well, alright, just for a short time, we need to be getting back to prepare your Uncle Malc's dinner soon," replied Great Aunty Dot, not wanting to deny them but wearying already at the thought of climbing the hill to the tower.

At the top of the hill, the children ran around the base of the old tower. "Aaaaaggghh, what's that on the roof?" Seth screamed.

Looking up at the roof, his great aunt could see he was looking at a couple of gargoyles hanging over the rooftop.

"Oh, that's just a gargoyle. All the old buildings and churches have them. They were originally made as gutter drains and to ward off evil spirits, but some of them look quite frightening and evil themselves," explained Aunty Dot.

Around the building, Pacey found a metal inscription on the wall. "What's this, Aunty?" she asked.

"Oh, that's a plaque commemorating the building and the people who worked on it."

"What's a 'P.L.A.K', and 'com memor hating'?" Seth puzzled.

"It's a 'plaque'" – Aunty Dot laughed – "which is just another word for a sign and it's 'commemorating', which is another word for remembering or honouring the people who worked on the building and the reason why it was built."

"She uses big words a lot," whispered Seth to Solomon.

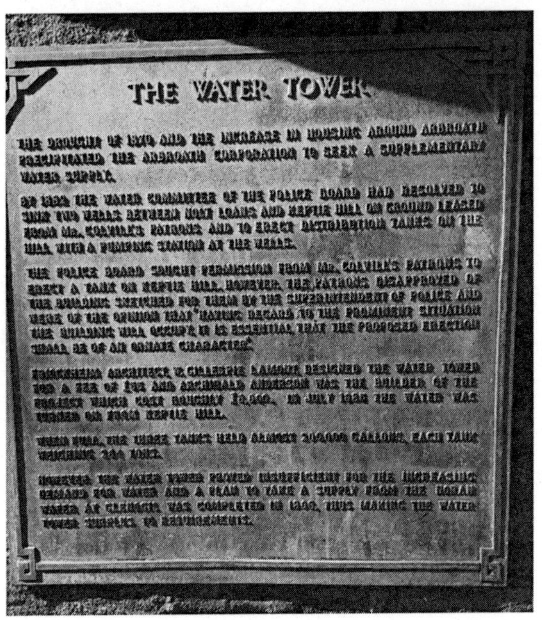

The three children, happy that they had explored all they could, went back with their great aunt to the house to get ready for dinner.

At the dinner table, all three were desperate to tell their great uncle all about what they had done that day.

"Ah yes, the water tower, a great building in its day and still is, I dare say," commented Uncle Malc. "Of course, there are stories that the building is haunted and that on a still night you can hear the voices of the men trapped in the tunnels below where a tunnel caved in."

"Malcolm," barked Great Aunty Dot, "what did I tell you! The kids are almost ready for bed, and we don't want any nightmares, do we? If so, YOU will be the one dealing with it."

Undeterred, Great Uncle Malc went on. "Some folks say that there are hidden passageways under the tower and that there is gold or diamonds or something like that found when they were digging out the waterways. The rumour was that the old builder Cedric Anderson had found some Celtic treasure when they were digging the original tunnels for the waterways. After the treasure was found, he started digging additional tunnels in the pretext it was for the waterways, but he was just using it as a ruse to hide what he was up to. He had the soil removed to his quarry where he could sift for gold or diamonds without anyone knowing. He needed to keep it secret as he was frightened that if the council found out, they would claim it for the town. Once he was sure he had taken most of the treasure out of the hill, he had it buried in one of the secret tunnels. He meant to come back for it someday, but he died shortly after the building was finished and as far as the legend goes, it still lies there undiscovered. Some say that Old Cedric left a secret sign or a map as to where he hid the treasure, but no one has ever found it. That's, of course, if there was ever any treasure in the first place, you know what people can be like. If they don't know, they make it up."

The three children's faces were a picture, all engrossed with this new tale of adventure and treasure and right on their doorstep.

"Of course, with all those ghosts and Old Cedric howling away in the tunnels looking for his treasure, it tends to keep most people away anyhow."

"For pity's sake, you have to go and overexaggerate your stories, you just can't help yourself, can you?" Great Aunty Dot huffed, exasperated. "Right, children, upstairs and get ready for bed, that's quite enough excitement for one day. I'll be up to read you a bedtime story tonight."

"Ohhh, but we want the Hobbit," cried Solomon.

"Very well, but ONLY the Hobbit…understand?" said Great Aunty Dot giving her husband one of her…looks.

"OK," said the threesome.

"As you say, dear." Great Uncle Malc chuckled.

After the second chapter of the Hobbit was finished and their uncle retired to the living room, three whisperers got to work under the blankets and all they could talk about was the water tower and the hidden treasure.

"Do you think Uncle Malc was telling us a fib about the treasure?" whispered Seth.

"And the ghosts?" said Solomon.

"Probably," chipped in Pacey with a grown-up air in her voice, pretending to know better. "Remember what Dad told us about his stories?"

"I suppose," said the other two bowing to her greater knowledge.

They went to sleep ages later as all three of them were excited to find out more about the tower, fib or no fib.

Chapter III
Lights in the Darkness

The next day, Sunday, was spent visiting some of the other aunties and uncles in the town who were desperate to see the children. The children were not quite so desperate as they wanted to go treasure hunting. However, once the aunties started to spoil them, they soon realised that treasure could be found closer to home and without as much effort. Toys, sweets and clothes were all around them. "It's almost like Christmas." Solomon whooped.

Monday, however, started poorly for the adventurers. The alarm did not go off and Uncle Malc was late for work.

Aunty Dot was suitably harassed getting her husband off to work with some breakfast inside him before trying to get the three tired visitors up, washed, dressed and fed.

As Solomon came down the stairs, he was chanting "Great Dotty Aunt, Great Dotty Aunt", laughing each time he repeated it. His great Aunt who heard him did not see the same funny side and gave him one of her famous looks. Seth however heard him and joined in the chanting. "Great Dotty Aunt, Great Dotty Aunt", getting louder as they went. Pacey heard the two of them from the top of the stairs and tried to quieten them down, but they only got louder and louder.

Having failed to turn the two chanters into stone with her looks, Aunty Dot turned on them. "Right, that's it, you three, there will be no going out today, you'll stay in and read your books or find something to play with from the toy box. Maybe then you will learn some respect," she thundered.

Great Aunty Dot was not normally so easily wound up, but she was flustered and had the beginnings of a migraine.

This punishment was, of course, met with a load of groans and moans but they had pushed their great aunt too far and she was not about to back down.

Pacey became resigned to the toy box, where she found some old picture books and puzzle books that used to belong to her father as his name was inside them. She settled down and started to work on them. The other two also went rummaging in the box and came up with some old Action Man dolls and toys which kept them amused for most of the remaining morning.

Pacey got engrossed in the types of word puzzles where you have to find words in any direction out of a scramble of letters just like the one below.

X	W	R	K	E	D
P	A	O	L	A	D
L	E	P	M	P	O
A	R	E	S	A	J
N	O	E	L	F	N
E	S	R	O	T	W

She managed to uncover the words: woman, rope, plane, peel and rot. *Is there any more?* she asked herself. Pacey found she loved this type of puzzle and could spend hour after hour doing them.

At lunchtime, Solomon asked, "If we are good, can we go back to the water tower tomorrow?"

"Yes, of course," replied Great Aunty Dot, feeling just a little ashamed that she had kept the children in all day.

"Perhaps you can take a rubbing of the water tower plaque to take back to your mum and dad," offered his Great Aunt.

"What's a rubbing, Aunty Dot?" asked Seth.

"Well, that's where you take a sheet of blank paper, hold it over the thing you want to copy and rub it with a soft pencil until it makes an outline of the item below it, just like the plaque," replied Aunty Dot. "Some people made it a hobby to take rubbings of gravestones."

She's as bad as Uncle Malc, thought Pacey.

However, the promise of a new activity seemed to keep them quiet for the rest of the day.

By six o'clock, Uncle Malc had come home and Aunty Dot was preparing dinner.

"What's for dinner tonight?" asked Solomon.

"Well, I thought you should have another Scottish dish again; so, I have made you all haggis, tatties and neeps," replied Aunty Dot.

"What's in that?" said Solomon with a screwed-up face.

"Just eat it and I'll tell you after, if you like it," said Aunty Dot.

They managed to eat most of the huge plateful that had been put in front of them. So, again the question was asked.

"That was quite nice Aunty Dot, but what's a 'haggis'?"

"Well, just sheep's brains, oatmeal, some offal, blood and held together in a pig's bladder." laughed Aunty Dot.

"Yeh, righto," said Pacey, "just like last night's stovies, you won't catch us out twice in a row. So, what is in it?"

"No," said Aunty Dot, "that's what's in it. Well, you did ask!"

"Really?"

"Really."

The three faces went four different shades of green.

"I think I'll go to bed," said Pacey.

That night Pacey could not sleep, she just tossed and turned. Whether it was the dinner or not is unknown, but she got up to look out of the window. All around was deathly silent and no traffic passing by which was slightly unusual however, it was one o'clock in the morning. Pacey looked out over the pond adjusting her eyes to the dark to see if she could see any of the ducks or swans. Then, something caught her eye. She looked up at the water tower and then, yes, it was a flash of light coming from the tower. She kept on looking and at the top of the tower, every now and again, there was a blue spark of light coming from the top.

What can that be? she asked herself and kept staring for over an hour. Eventually, the lights stopped. Pacey was in a muddle because part of her wanted to run into Aunty Dot's bedroom and tell her about the lights and the other half knew she would get a row for staying up so late when she should have been sleeping. Thinking better of it, she decided to tell her aunt in the morning.

The next morning, Pacey was the first one down at the breakfast table. "Aunty Dot, Aunty Dot, you'll never guess what I saw last night?" She gasped.

"Yes, yes Pacey, have your breakfast and tell me about it later," said Aunty Dot.

"But Aunty Dot it's…" went Pacey in reply but this was met by a Great Aunty Dot stare…Dogs began to bark.

One thing's for sure, Pacey was a quick learner and decided that she had better do as she was told.

A half plateful of cornflakes and a half glass of orange juice was thrown down Pacey's throat in record time. With barely a pause for breath, she tried blurting out again, "You'll never guess what I saw over at the pond, it was weird, there were lights and, and flashes and more lights and–"

"Yes, yes, dear, I told your great uncle this would happen with all his daft stories," said Aunty Dot.

"No, no, Aunty Dot, this was for real," cried Pacey.

"What's this?" Uncle Malc breezed as he sat down at the table.

"It's all your fault telling stories about ghosts just before sending them to bed." Aunty Dot glowered. Uncle Malc narrowly missed being turned to stone.

Pacey told her uncle all about the lights.

"Ah, at this time of the year you have probably seen the Aurora Borealis," said Uncle Malc.

"The 'ororo bori' what?" Pacey frowned.

"The 'Aurora' (Oro-ra) 'Borealis' (Bore-e-a-lis) is another name for the Northern Lights, Aurora from the Roman goddess of Dawn and Borealis from the Greek name 'Boreas' for North. It's all to do with magnetic pulses and emissions of photons in the Earth's upper atmosphere mixing with solar wind particles in the sky which emits a strange eerie light. The Cree Indians called them the 'Dance of the Spirits'.

Goodness, don't they teach anything at school these days?" said Uncle Malc, finally running out of steam.

The muttering of "Over egging again" was completely ignored by the uncle.

"No, no, this was different," cried Pacey.

"I don't think so, child," said Uncle Malc all patronisingly, "Listen to your uncle, how would you know it was different if you haven't seen an Aurora Borealis?" With that, he was off to work kissing his wife on the way out the door.

Uncle Malc's logic was right, but Pacey was not convinced and decided to investigate for herself later on.

Chapter IV
The Secret Message

All through breakfast Pacey could hardly contain herself and took all her powers to stay calm. Once all the dishes were put away and the rest of the children cleaned and dressed, Aunty Dot proclaimed, "Right children, I promised you that I would take you to the tower to take a rubbing but look" – she pointed outside, the rain was beginning to pelt down – "no point going now, the paper will get soaked, instead, we will go down to the lighthouse museum." Paccy was devastated.

The day dragged and dragged. Aunty Dot tried to make the lighthouse museum as interesting as possible which satisfied Seth and Solomon, but Pacey hardly heard a word.

The evening meal was torture. Once in bed, Pacey lay awake until all was quiet and the other two were fast asleep. Up to her window, she clambered and looked over at the water tower, looking for those mysterious lights.

Nothing. Pacey looked at her watch, 12:15.

In her head, half an hour passed.

Nothing.

Another half hour passed.

Nothing.

She looked at her watch and it read: 12:45. Time drags when you are waiting for something to happen.

She was all ready to turn in, disappointed that she must have imagined the lights. Or maybe, just maybe, her great uncle was right. No, that can't be.

Just as she turned to go back to bed, a slither of blue light emerged from the darkness. There it was, the blue lights, then darkness, then a spurt of blue light, nothing, blue lights. On and on they went for about ten minutes, then off for good.

Right, thought Pacey.

The next day, Pacey was beside herself. She was up first and setting up the breakfast table before even her great aunt was up. "My, my, young lady, what's got into you today?" said Aunty Dot with surprise.

"Oh nothing, I just wanted to help," replied, the less-than-honest Pacey.

After breakfast, Pacey cleared the plates and put them into the dishwasher. Yes, Great Aunty Dot was posh.

"OK, young people, what will we do today?" expressed Aunty Dot.

"Let's go back to the museum," an excited Seth shouted.

"Owh." a surprised Seth howled after Pacey had kicked his shin.

"You said you would take us to the tower to do a rubbing so that we could send them to Mum and Dad," said an innocent Pacey.

"So I did," said Aunty Dot, "and a promise is a promise."

Aunty Dot found three sheets of A3 paper from Uncle Malc's office desk and three soft pencils from his art box. "Not a word now as to where these came from," said the felonious Aunty Dot.

All armed with the necessary tools, the threesome ran up the hill towards the water tower.

"Can I go first?" Seth puffed at the top of the hill.

"You are the youngest," said Pacey, "and so, no. Me first, I'm the oldest."

"Pacey," said Aunty Dot with a stare over her glasses.

Birds dropped out the sky.

"Oh OK." Pacey grumped, "but he'll make a mess of it…"

And a mess of it he made. The pencil was gripped too hard, and he rubbed so vigorously that the pencil went through the paper more than once. Solomon was a bit more patient and saw where Seth went wrong, but still his efforts were not that recognisable as to the words on the plaque. Pacey was determined that she would get it just right and followed her aunt's instructions to the letter. "Not too hard, dear," encouraged her great aunt.

At last, a pencil version of the plaque came into view on the paper.

"Wonderful, dear," said Great Aunty Dot, "although you have rubbed a little bit too hard over some letters." There was evidence that some of the letters were a lot darker than the others.

"But these are the letters, Aunty Dot, some are higher than others," complained Pacey.

"Yes dear," said Great Aunty Dot, not looking for an argument.

Back at the house, Pacey went to her bedroom to admire her work. "OK kids, how about writing a letter to your mum and dad and sending your plaque rubbings with it? I'm sure they will be impressed," shouted up Great Aunty Dot.

Laid out on the floor, Pacey stared at her endeavours. *Looks pretty good to me,* thought Pacey, *better than the other two anyway.*

As she looked, she noticed what her great Aunty was talking about. Some of the letters did show up darker than the others. *That's a pity,* she thought. Then she noticed that some of them made words: 1870, SEEK, KEPTIE, HILL. Then: AND, IS, L, TH, R, NO, ARDS, Y; along with some other random letters.

Hmmm, thought Pacey and then was interrupted by Great Aunty Dot calling up, telling them to get washed up for dinner.

After dinner, Pacey occupied herself by working through her puzzle book. After a few puzzles, she did another one of the random word puzzles that she liked to do. After completing the puzzle, she looked over at the rubbing on the floor. *I wonder,* she thought *I wonder, could this be a similar puzzle?*

"Time for bed, kids," called out Uncle Malc, "come on now, beddy byes."

"Beddy byes." Solomon sniggered, "who says that anymore? That's so yesterday."

All three changed for bed without argument, although one of them had other plans.

Under the blanket Pacey had hidden a small torch and was busy trying to decipher the rubbings secrets.

"What's all this then?" said Uncle Malc.

"What's all what?" replied a startled Pacey.

Then she looked down and saw the rubbing and all her workings strewn about the floor as she had fallen asleep still trying to puzzle out the letters.

"Oh, it's nothing, Uncle Malc, I thought I could see a hidden meaning in the rubbing I took yesterday."

"Let's see, then," said Uncle Malc, "I used to be good at this sort of thing." Pacey was not amused.

"Hhmm, maybe you are on to something, youngster. These letters ESTNRTHOA could make 'North-east'. These other letters ARDYS could make 'Yards'. So, with what you've got already, it could be: 'Seek 1870 yards from the water sink at Keptie Hill, North-east to…' what other letters do you have left, oh, I see 'DISLAN'. Now, there is a Dishlandtown street in the town, have you got another D and an H? There's bound to be a 'TOWN' in the letters?"

"No," said Pacey, secretly happy that her great uncle had put together so many bits of the jigsaw.

"Oh well, I'm off to do some home-work, good luck with your secret message." Uncle Malc laughed as he whistled out the door, kissing Great Aunty Dot on the way.

"They're always kissing," said Seth.

"Yeh, yuk," replied Solomon, "Too old or what?"

The air went cold as they turned around to find one of Great Aunty Dots stares bleaching them white.

"I heard that, young man, let me tell you, you are never too old for a bit of lovey dovey," she said as she turned around to hide a smirk, leaving two young men with their mouths open.

"And close your mouths, you are not a fly trap," she said as she went into the living room.

"How does she do that?" questioned Solomon. "How does she see out of the back of her head?"

"I heard that too," came the voice from the living room.

Silence.

Chapter V
The Elephant Man

All day Pacey could not concentrate on anything else except the secret message. At one point, she was going to share it with the others but that was not an option.

She was going to share it with her great aunty but she didn't want to do that either.

"Come on," shouted Seth and Solomon together, "let's go exploring the gardens. We're going to be pirates and play Peter Pan, you can be Wendy. The middle of the garden can be the island."

"I don't want to be Wendy on your stupid Island." Pacey grumped.

A penny dropped from somewhere.

"That's it, that's it. It's not 'Dishland', it's 'ISLAND', the island on the pond. Thank you, boys, thank you." Pacey screamed as she kissed both of them on the forehead and ran back to her bedroom.

"This kissing game is catching," said Seth rubbing the kiss off like a touch of the plague.

Back in the bedroom, Pacey laid out her words.

'Seek 1870 yards from the water sink at Keptie Hill Northeast to the Island.'

That night, Pacey made up her mind to go up to the water tower and check her revelation out. By tomorrow, she could be a millionaire.

There was a hitch though, there was no way to tell her which way was North-east and no way to indicate 1870 yards.

"Aunty Dot."

"Yes Pacey."

"Does Uncle Malc have a compass?"

"Not that I know of."

That's not the answer Pacey wanted. New tact.

"Aunty Dot."

"Yes Pacey."

"Can I get an advance on my pocket money?"

"Why?"

"Nothing, really."

"Well, if it's nothing, you won't need an advance."

She is too smart for her own good, thought Pacey.

New tact.

"Well, I was thinking that if Uncle Malc doesn't have a compass then maybe I could buy him one as a thank you gift for reading the Hobbit to us."

"That's nice dear, but what would Uncle Malc need with a compass?"

Oh, give in, why don't you? thought Pacey.

"Perhaps he could show us where the North Star is or point to which direction Mum and Dad went," said Pacey in desperation.

"Oh, that's lovely," said Aunty Dot, "I think that's a very nice idea, we will buy one tomorrow. There will be no need to bring forward your pocket money, let's consider it a treat for Uncle Malc's hard work."

You beauty, thought Pacey, but replied, *thank you very much Aunty Dot, that's really good of you.*

That night, Pacey went to sleep with all sorts of things going through her brain. After she had been asleep for what seemed like hours, she woke up bolt upright. It was only 12:30. She was drawn to the window for some reason. As she approached, the breath from her lips started to fog over the window, enough that she had to wipe the window clear. It was getting frosty now. There it was, blue sparks of light coming from the water tower.

Right, she thought.

Putting on her thickest tights and woolliest jumper, she started to creep out of her room. *Creeeaaaakkk,* went the floorboards as she stepped out onto the landing. She paused, holding her breath. *Great, no one heard,* thought Pacey. Off she went down the landing. One foot after the other, right to the start of the stairs. Hold breath.

Quiet.

"Good, let's go."

"Where are you going?" whispered Seth.

"Shhsss, go back to bed," whispered back Pacey.

"But I want to come," whined Seth. His voice getting louder.

"Oh, all right, but keep quiet and get some warm clothes on, it's freezing outside," said Pacey in a hushed voice, thinking it was better to take Seth with her than start a commotion outside their aunty and uncle's bedroom.

"Can I come as well?" said the third sleepy voice belonging to Solomon.

"Oh, all right, but be quick and put some warm clothes on."

Outside, the three adventurers ran across the road towards the water tower. Up the hill they went, slowing down as they got nearer the blue lights.

"What are we doing here?" cried Seth. "I'm freezing."

"Yes, this is daft, I'm telling Aunty Dot tomorrow," cried Solomon in support of his brother.

"Look, you two, I only allowed you two to come because I didn't want you to wake up Uncle Malc and Aunty Dot. Can you imagine how cross they would be to find you pair out of bed, never mind outside in this weather. I'll say that I came after you to bring you back," said a desperate Pacey.

The two brothers looked at each other and knew they were beaten. Just by that, blue lights started to emerge from the outside door of the tower.

Curiosity drew them forward, all three of them were scared stiff.

Pacey slowly and quietly opened the door. The door gave a small creak as it opened but there was no reaction from inside.

Slowly, the three adventurers crept into the doorway. Inside there was another door with an opaque glass window. Sparking blue light could be seen coming through the window. They edged closer to the door and there it was. A strange dark figure with blue lights and sparks coming from his hands. Smoke was also coming from his hands and there was a metallic smell going up their noses.

A desk was behind the door with a frosted glass window which hid their presence from whatever was causing the light.

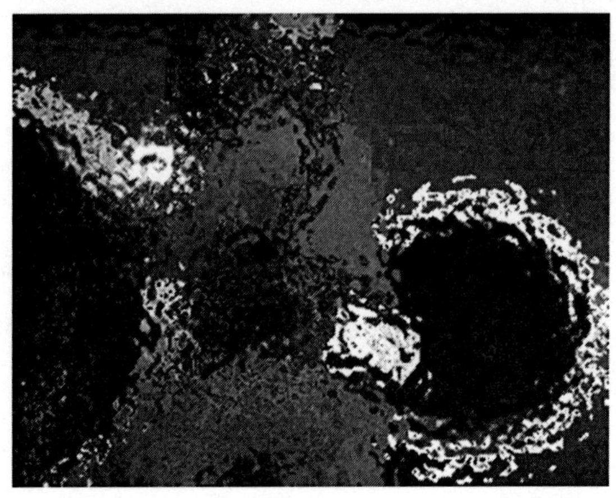

"Now, be very, very quiet, you two," said Pacey in a very hushed tone. They crept in the doorway behind a bench at the door. All three little heads, one by one started to rise over the bench.

The three were no longer brave adventurers. Their brains had just melted and all three had 'an accident'. Their jaws were wide open as they looked upon this strange alien-like figure. Seth gasped and the figure stopped what he was doing.

The three heads dropped down below the bench. Pacey looked around the side of the bench. Solomon looked around the other side. They all held their breaths.

The figure had just started to resume his work when Seth, who couldn't take it anymore, ran for the door kicking a plate of metal over as he went. Immediately, the figure turned around and caught sight of the remaining two.

What was worse was that the remaining two caught sight of the figure as it turned around. Its head had two huge eyes and was covered in a mask. From the bottom of it drooped a large trunk and its breathing sounded like Darth Vader out of Star Wars.

"Elephant Man," cried Pacey and Solomon in unison.

"Aaaaagggggghhhh," they cried as they ran for the door with Elephant Man hot in pursuit.

On and on they ran, too frightened to look back until they were at the foot of the hill.

When they did, they saw a tall figure in the darkness looking down at them. Worse still, he was pointing at them.

Nothing could stop the three from running straight back to their aunty.

"Aaaaagggggghhh, aaaaggghhh," they cried as they ran into the sanctuary of their great aunty and uncle's house.

"Aaaaagggggghhh, aaaaggghhh."

"What in the devil?" cried out Uncle Malc as he opened his bedroom door.

"Aliens, Aliens," cried out Solomon.

"Elephant Man, Elephant Man," cried out Pacey.

"It's Pacey's fault," blurted out Seth, now starting to cry.

"Right, you three, what in God's name are you three doing outside at this time of night?" screamed a very angry Aunty Dot.

"Pacey!"

"Yes Aunty."

"Well?"

"What?"

"I'm waiting."

"Well, you wouldn't believe me about the lights and they were there again tonight. So I went to see what was causing them. Solomon and Seth would have clipped on me if I didn't take them with me, it wasn't my idea," blurted out Pacey.

"It's one thirty in the morning, I'll deal with you three tomorrow, now get to bed and If I hear one whisper, well, I wouldn't like to be that person," threatened Aunty Dot.

"Now, BED."

There was no argument, each wondering what pain would be inflicted tomorrow. All that Seth and Solomon knew was that Pacey was to blame. No question.

Chapter VI
Distance Is a Problem

"Right, you three, what am I going to do with you?" said a very irate Great Aunty Dot. "Your uncle went up to the water tower before he went to work and everything was as it should be. There were no signs of life and no signs of anyone having entered the tower. It was starting to snow and he was not pleased, I can tell you, having been sent on a wild goose chase. You are all just too hyper. You have had too many stories and it's making you imagine all sorts, so no more Hobbits."

"Oh, Aunty Dot," the three chimed in unison. "Please, please, please, we'll be good, honest. Bilbo has just gone into the cave and met Gollum."

"I'll Gollum you," came the reply, followed by a silence no one wanted to break…if they knew what was good for them.

Unfortunately, Pacey didn't know what was good for her.

"We'll just be off to the park then, Aunty," she said, a bit too cocky.

"Indeed, you will not, you will stay right here where I can keep an eye on you all."

The rest of the day was played out in near silence.

However, as most adults do, Great Aunty Dot began to feel a little guilty for keeping them inside even though the weather was changing.

"Right, you lot, coats on and be quick about it, I have some errands to get for tea tonight," said Aunty Dot, surprising the adventurers into action.

Their coats and shoes were on in no time and they were standing at the door awaiting the next command.

The shops were only a few minutes' walk into the centre of the town and the fresh air was putting a red glow on their cheeks. A few forays into various shops for mundane items was made without comment. Hopes for any venture into toy shops were fast diminishing.

As they were approaching the centre of the high street, Aunty Dot stopped and turned to Pacey. "Mmmhh, I seem to recall you wanted to buy Uncle Malc a compass, did you not? The Jewellers have several in the window, I can see. Go and choose one Pacey, if you would. As for you two, go into Haags shop, they have a toy counter at the back."

The speed of sound could be measured by the time it took all three to reach their destinations. Aunty Dot stood looking after them with a smirk on her face, possibly remembering similar misdemeanours in her past.

"This looks like a nice one, Aunty Dot," said Pacey, "and it's not too pricey." She pointed to a brass-encased compass in a leather pouch.

"Agreed, let's go in and buy it. We will keep it a secret until the week-end, no doubt he will need a bit of cheering up by then."

Pacey didn't ask why, no need to push it.

Toys were bought for all three. Seth had a new batman Lego, Solomon bought a magic game and Pacey came away with some beads for making necklaces and shapes.

The three were quite content to spend the rest of the day playing with their toys and no mention was made of going outside.

Teatime was a similarly quiet affair when Uncle Malc got home. The silence at the table was broken when Uncle Malc said, "I went to the council today to make inquiries about the tower to see if there was anyone working at it. I spoke with a very nice young man called 'Ralph' who was in charge of planning permits. It seems someone did put in an offer to buy it quite recently and wanted to turn it into a diving school, or so they said. I can't imagine how that would work. There is no road up to it and it's a public right of way. Anyway, the application was rejected and they said that there was no one working at it. I did say that my great niece saw some lights coming from it at night, but he said that was impossible, it's all locked up. So that's that then, young Pacey."

"But…" started Solomon who was immediately silenced with a swift kick to the shins from Pacey. "Nothing…" he mumbled, "please may I leave the table."

"Well, you can't take it with you." Uncle Malc laughed.

"MALCOLM."

"Yes, of course you can, Solomon," said Aunty Dot, "Nice to hear that someone has manners around here." A cold wind swept through the room.

The next day, the children were allowed to take a ball over beside the pond where there was some goal posts; with a reminder to stay away from the water and the tower.

As well as carrying the ball, Pacey had another item in her pocket!

After about an hour of playing football, Pacey announced she was going to run up the hill. The other two looked at the steep hill and decided to let her go on her own.

Once up at the top, she was standing at the fence that surrounded the tower immediately in front of the old water trough (or sink). "Right, I am about three yards from the sink." Out of her pocket, she took Great Uncle Malc's compass. The needle swung around and Pacey aligned the compass with North. North-east was pointing right to the biggest tree on the pond's Island. *Great,* she thought, *I just need to keep a straight line with that tree and I will know where the treasure is.*

Off she trotted, trying to measure out each step as she went. She had previously taken a measure of her stride and knew that each step would be two feet. As she approached the edge of the pond, she had counted 970 steps. Pacey took her mobile phone out and used the calculator. 970 steps x 2 feet = 1940 feet. 1940 divided by 3 = 646 yards. *That's not right,* she thought, *it must be in the Island, the plaque clearly said 1870.*

Then another problem settled in her head. *How was she to get to the island across the water?*

Pacey was crestfallen, her big adventure coming to an even bigger end. What now?

At the dinner table, Great Aunty Dot said, "You are awfully quiet for once Pacey, are you OK?"

"Yes fine, just tired," she answered.

The two brothers took this as an opportunity to be the centre stage and started talking away, ninety to the dozen. All of which just made Pacey's mood drop even further.

"I'm off to bed," said Pacey, leaving the rest of the room stunned into silence at her departure.

Once in her room, she lifted clothes up and put them down again, threw some soft toys across the room and threw herself backwards on to the bed. Looking across the bed, she saw the rubbing of the plaque sitting on the bedside table. With that she got up, tore it in half, scrunched it up and threw it in the bin. "Stupid, stupid, stupid idea." She huffed and threw herself back on the bed.

Aunty Dot entered.

"Pacey, what's going on? Why did you tear up your rubbing? I thought you were going to send it to your mum and dad. Are you not feeling well?" said a concerned Aunty Dot.

The mention of Mum and Dad brought her back into the room.

"Oh, I forgot," said Pacey with a trembling lip. "It was a stupid idea, thinking I could solve a mystery after all those years."

"Never mind," comforted Aunty Dot, "you had some fun trying to work it out, didn't you? It was an adventure of sorts and you never know, you might have solved it. Tomorrow we will go back up to the tower and you can take another rubbing for your mum and dad."

Uncle Malc was about to read the next chapter of the Hobbit. Things were heating up. Bilbo had found the magic ring and they were on the way to fight Smaug the dragon. Pacey did not want to miss this episode and her mood lightened as she drifted through to her brother's bedroom.

The next day, Aunty Dot was as good as her word and took Pacey up to the tower for another rubbing. They had to work quickly as it was beginning to get very cold and they had to wrap up well.

Pacey was a bit more careful this time and made a far better job of taking the rubbing and was pleased with the outcome.

Back at the house, Pacey went to fold the rubbing up to be able to post it to her parents.

Just as she was folding it, her eyes glanced over it once more and with a shrug and a large sigh she started folding. Then her eyes caught the numbers 1870. The number '1' was quite faint compared to the other numbers and it now looked like '870'. *Wait a minute,* she thought, *just wait a minute.* What if the real distance was 870 and not 1870? If you allow the distance from the edge of the pond to the island and the extra few feet from the edge of the fence to the sink, that can't be far off 870 yards.

All of a sudden, the old Pacey was back. Problem one sorted.

Chapter VII
A Cold Snap

The second problem, of course, now, was how to get across to the island. The pond was not that deep but deep enough to drown a small child. Pacey couldn't swim and how would she explain her wet clothes to her Great Aunty Dot. She did not want to get in her bad books…again.

In the morning, Pacey and the other two boys rose for breakfast. The first thing they noticed was how chilly it had become.

"Right, you three, get some warm porridge down you, we are in for a cold spell and you will need to get something nourishing and warm inside you," said Great Aunty Dot.

Porridge was not the first choice on the three's menu, but with a little sugar and milk, they soon gulped it down.

"Now while I clear up, why don't you get some warm clothes on and go into the garden and play for a bit," said their Aunty.

Once outside as they started to play, they heard some noises from next door. It turned out to be two girls.

"What's your name?" said Pacey.

The two girls were startled for a bit as they were not used to seeing young people in their neighbours' garden.

"I'm Nia," said the oldest one, "and that's my little sister Tara. What are you doing in Mr Turner's garden?"

"We are just staying with our great uncle and aunty until my dad and mum come back from a business trip in America," said Pacey.

"Well, we were just going to play on our bouncy trampoline. Do you want to join us?" said a kind Nia.

"Cool," went three voices.

The five children played for an hour on the trampoline until Pacey noticed a small pink dingy lying inside Nia and Tara's Wendy House.

"That's a nice dingy you have there," said Pacey, "have you ever tried using it across at the pond?"

"No," said Nia, "we got it for Christmas last year, but we have only used it at the swimming baths."

"Do you fancy trying it out?" an excited Pacey blurted out.

"I don't think my mum would be too happy," replied a nervous Tara.

"Oh, come on, let's try," said Pacey "you're not scared, are you?"

Not wanting to seem wimpish, Nia said, "Well, alright then, but just for a little while."

"I'm telling Mum," said Tara.

Nia picked up the dingy and paddle and strutted to the gate. "Go ahead, see if I care," she replied.

Just as they were rounding the corner of the house, a big brown dog came bounding up to them, scaring the living daylights out of the three visitors.

The dog was running circles around them, barking like mad and jumping up on them, licking their faces.

"Roo, get down," said a man's voice.

"Hi Dad," said Nia.

"Where are you off to, you lot, and who is this you have with you?" said Glen, who was Nia and Tara's father. Glen had just come back from taking Roo for a walk.

"This is Mr and Mrs Turner's niece and nephews, up for a few weeks' holiday. We were just going over the road to the pond."

"Indeed, you are not," said Glen, "what made you think you can go to the pond without me or your mum with you? You know it's dangerous, don't you? Right inside now, say goodbye to your new friends, you can see them tomorrow." "Nice to meet you, I hope you have a nice stay," Glen said to the three visitors as he headed inside the house.

Nia and Tara followed, taking with them the dingy and Pacey's hope of getting across to the island.

'Ooooooooh, buuuuummer.' Pacey screamed in her head as she headed back to their house. As she went, she noticed that now they had stopped playing, her hands were very cold and her nose was red. The two boys were also starting to shiver.

Inside, they heated themselves up with some hot juice Great Aunty Dot had made. Pacey was stumped for an idea as how to get across to the island and for the time being, she contented herself by playing games with Solomon and Seth.

When Uncle Malc came home, he was rubbing his hands and blowing on them. "Goodness, it is cold tonight, I wouldn't be surprised if the pond doesn't freeze over tonight." He remarked.

A certain little lady's ears picked up.

"Really, Uncle Malc?"

"Well, it is cold enough, however, be warned, the ice will be very thin, so do not even think about playing on it. It will take at least three days of this type of frost to make it safe to bear the weight of anyone."

That night, Pacey paid very close attention to the weather reports on the T.V. The stars were in her favour as the weekly report indicated that the cold snap was likely to last through to the weekend.

Chapter VIII
The Island

The next three days dragged for Pacey. That was until she was wakened by Seth on the third day. "Get up, get up, get up." an excited Seth screamed, "it's been snowing all night. Let's go out and play snowballs."

Pacey wiped her eyes and slowly made her way to the bedroom window. All around was white. Her eyes widened. It was all she could do to stop herself dashing out the door and running over the road to the island. However, she knew that she would be in deep trouble if she did. So, unusually for her, she casually got washed and dressed before going downstairs for breakfast.

"Hello, sleepyhead." Aunty Dot laughed. "I thought you would be up and hounding me to get out to the snow."

"Not bothered," came the reply.

"Oh right, well, grumpy, eat your porridge, drink your tea and then brush your teeth," said Aunty Dot huffily.

The problem now would be to get to the island without anyone knowing…especially Aunty Dot knowing about it. It would have to be done at night again. However, that would not be easy and if she was caught, she knew she would be grounded…for life!

The rest of the day dragged and was spent building a snowman with Seth, Nia and Tara. Solomon had started to sniffle with a cold and was kept inside by Aunty Dot.

That night, once everyone was tucked up in bed and the sound of snoring could be heard coming from her aunt and uncle's room (she never could figure out who was snoring), Pacey collected her things.

"A torch, Check! Compass, Check! Tape rule, Check!

Rope, oh well, a clothes line will have to do, Check!"

Silently, she crept out the bedroom, past her aunt and uncle's bedroom, across the hall and very, very, quietly down the staircase. Outside it was freezing, with a slight dusting of snowfall. *At least that will cover my tracks*, she thought.

At the pond, she took her eye-line from the tower to the largest tree on the island and started to walk towards it. One foot on the ice and it gave a small creaking noise. All of a sudden, doubts came into her head. *What if I fall in, there will be no one to save me.* However, the thought of all those riches at the island spurred her on.

Just as she put her second foot on the ice, the ice splintered and gave another noisier creak. A hand went on her shoulder.

Pacey just about had another 'accident', as well as a heart attack. Her legs gave way as she turned around to face her attacker.

"I knew you were up to something, lady!"

"SETH! You nearly gave me a heart attack, you little brat, what are you doing here?"

"I knew you were up to something," said Seth, "you have been far too quiet these last few days. I thought you would try something like this."

"Oh you little…oh, I could," loudly whispered Pacey, but secretly she was pleased she had someone else with her.

The pair made their advances over to the island, one careful foot after another. Creak, splinter, creak, splinter went the ice as they made their way over.

Once over, Pacey got her bearings and started to count the remaining steps to the middle of the island. "Right," she said to Seth, "it must be around here somewhere. You look over there and I'll look back here," she said.

For all she tried, she could not see anything that looked promising. Seth was also having trouble as he did not have a torch with him, so it was doubly hard for him.

As Seth crept around towards the large tree, there was a big bush in front of him. He pulled the leaves back and all of a sudden, there was an enormous beast in front of him, with wings eight feet wide charging at him. The beast started squawking louder and louder, its wings beating him and its long neck trying to bite him.

"Aaaahhh, save me," cried Seth as he backed away from the beast, frightened to turn his back on it. It was in the moonlight that he caught a good look at the animal and suddenly realised he had stumbled on a large swan's nest.

The swan kept charging at Seth with its wings beating him and its long neck pecking at him, bruising his arms and legs. Seth frantically backed away, tripped and fell backwards. There was a sound of breaking wood as he fell through a hole in the ground.

As he fell, he cried out for help. Pacey, hearing the screams ran towards the noise only to be confronted with the swan who had decided to turn on her.

"Shoo," she shouted and did the only thing she could think of and turned the torch beam straight at the swan. The swan backed off a little but was still hissing at her and darting its neck at her legs.

"Help me, Pacey," cried Seth from below.

"Yes!" Pacey whooped. "Well done for finding the secret tunnel," not thinking whether her little brother was hurt.

"My leg hurts, Pacey," whimpered Seth.

"How far down are you?" said Pacey.

Pacey shone the torch down the hole and could just see her little brother's head in the darkness. As she turned the torch around, she saw there was a rough ladder cut into the face of the hole. Tying herself to the big tree with the clothesline that she had taken with her, she slowly lowered herself into the hole.

"Hurry, Pacey, my leg is hurting and I'm scared in the dark," said Seth as he started to cry.

"Stop being a woose," was her reply.

At the bottom, which was about fifteen feet down, Seth was lying on the ground. His leg and hands were bleeding. "Can you stand up?" asked Pacey.

"I don't know, everything hurts," said Seth.

"Well, try, we need to get you out of here," said Pacey with a bit of panic in her voice. She knew she was in deep, deep trouble if she could not get Seth back to the surface.

Seth stood up cautiously and managed to put his full weight on his legs. However, as he looked at the climb above him, he said, "I can't climb that far Pacey, it's too high."

Pacey in her heart of hearts knew he was right as she had struggled to climb down, the climb back up would be much harder and she did not have any wounds or bruises. She shone her torch around the hole and although it expanded out further, there was no way out.

Pacey slumped down and put her head in her hands. *I'm done for, now*, she thought.

Chapter IX
Seth Finds the Way

Tears began to well up in Pacey's eyes. Meanwhile, Seth had picked himself up knowing that nothing was broken. He picked up the torch that Pacey had lain down on the ground. As he shone it around, he immediately noticed two red eyes staring back at him. "Aaaaahhhhyyeee." He screamed out. Pacey lifted her head and looked at where the torch was shining. "Aaaaahhhyyeee." She screamed and both the children clung to each other.

The red eyes started to come towards them very slowly. There was a sound of sniffing.

As it came closer, its full body came into view.

"It's a rat, it's a rat," shouted Seth.

It was a large rat and as it got closer, it could smell the blood on Seth's hands and knees. Closer and closer it came, baring its large teeth and sprang at poor Seth.

He bent down and picked up a large stone and threw it as hard as he could at the rat. It scurried away before the stone could hit it.

"Phew, that was close," he said, "I hate rats."

He shone the torch to where the rat ran away but it was gone.

"Hang on," he said, "where did he go and how did he get down here?"

Pacey was still feeling sorry for herself and did not respond.

Seth made his way down to where the rat went and came against a hard wall. *Hmmphh, no way out here*, he thought. He turned around and laid against the wall and as he did, it gave a small creak. *Hello*, he thought, *walls don't creak*. He turned the torch about and scanned the wall. At the bottom near the floor, there was a small hole. He bent down and put his hand in the hole and grabbed the edge and pulled hard. Immediately, he tumbled backwards, landing on his already-sore bottom. He looked up and in his hand was a lump of wood. "Look Pacey, there's a door."

Pacey looked up and scrambled towards him.

"Oh, you lovely, lovely boy," she said and kissed his head.

"Get off." Seth shrugged, secretly liking that he had found a way out.

They both set about tearing at the doorway until they had made a big enough hole for them to crawl through.

"Where do you think it leads?" said Seth.

"I don't know, obviously, dummy," a sarcastic Pacey spat, who had now received her second wind now that there was a possible way out.

She shone her torch down the tunnel and all she could see was more darkness.

"Hang on," she said as she pulled out the compass from her pocket. The needle started to jump around but settled on South. *This is taking us back where we came from*, she thought. So down the tunnel they slowly went, being very careful not to meet the rat or its brothers and sisters.

Pacey had started to keep a rough count of the number of steps they had taken. That's about 1200 steps we've taken and calculated that that was 2400 feet, 800 yards. Pacey had always been good at arithmetic. "We must be just about under the tower," she said to Seth.

"So," replied Seth, "how do we get out of here?"

As they went deeper, the tunnel began to open out to a large round area and at its centre was a large wooden trunk. "Seth, Seth, I've found it, the missing treasure, I've found it."

"We've found it." Seth returned.

"Yeh, yeh, whatever." His sister fired back.

They both ran towards the trunk and started to open it when the torch went out.

Chapter X
The Return of the Elephant Man

In the dark, the two children grabbed on to each other. Pacey shook the torch and it went on, then immediately off again. Things were not looking good.

Seth and Pacey sat down on the trunk, heads on hands. Pacey decided to open the trunk, just to see if there was any treasure and to see if there was anything in there they could use.

They slowly opened the trunk and in went their hands.

Nothing! Well, almost nothing, just a single solid lump of stone.

Not a single item could they find.

They both slumped back down again.

Tears were within a millisecond of arriving. No treasure, no light, no one to help them.

Through the blur of tears, Pacey's eyes began to get used to the total darkness. And yet, there was no total darkness.

Ten feet away, there was a slight wave of light about three feet long on the ground.

Gradually, they crawled towards the light. It was the bottom edge of a door and what's more, there was someone on the other side.

What to do now? If they went in, there was a good chance the elephant man would be there. If they didn't go in, they would be trapped down in the tunnel…and in the dark.

Pacey felt around the door for some type of handle until she found something which felt like a latch. Slowly, she lifted it, trying to make as little noise as possible.

The door opened with a slight shove. 'Creeeeaakk' went the door. Pacey poked her head through the space, followed by Seth. There was no one there. Looking around, there was a small table and a set of stairs going upwards.

"This must take us up to the water tower," whispered Pacey, "stay very, very quiet."

Carefully, they edged their way upwards. At the top of the stairs was another doorway, only this time, it was made of metal. Pacey opened the door very carefully.

Creeeaaak.

Deafening!

Things went very quickly after that.

In front of them stood…the elephant man!

Wrong! As he swung around at the sound of the door, she saw there were two elephant men!

The men made a dash for them.

Pacey whipped around, grabbing Seth and made for the tunnel. They got through the first room where the casket was, Seth was now struggling as he had an injured leg. They were back in darkness again, although there was faint light coming from the elephant men following close behind them.

"Come on, Seth, we must try and get back to the hole and the ladder," cried Pacey with panic in her voice.

Just then, Seth fell, tripping over an old tree root.

The elephant men were almost on them.

"Run, Pacey, save yourself, get help," cried Seth bravely.

Just then, one of the elephant men had Seth by the collar.

Pacey turned and ran towards the hole and the ladder.

All she heard were the screams of Seth as he was dragged backwards and the feet of the other elephant man following close behind her.

At last, she got to the bottom of the hole and found the rough ladder.

Pacey jumped and grabbed on to one of the ladder rungs. Then she lifted her leg and managed to get a purchase on a rock or stone and shoved herself up. One rung at a time, she lifted herself up. Two more rungs and she was at the top.

Just as she got to the top of the hole and was about to crawl out, a hand grabbed her leg and pulled. Pacey did not have the strength to cling on and she fell, into the hands of elephant man. She was done for!

Chapter XI
Uncle Malc to the Rescue

Pacey looked around as her eyes began to focus. She couldn't move as her hands and legs were tied up. She couldn't speak as her mouth was gagged. She looked around and there was poor Seth, tied up the same as she was and lying on his side whimpering.

It was dark with only a glow of light coming from the other part of the tunnel. She figured that she was back in the room at the tower.

She had no idea how long she had been tied up, but it seemed like an age. She was now reflecting on her stupidity and how much trouble she was in…LOTS!

Tears began to roll down her face, she couldn't even make eye-contact with Seth to at least let him know she was with him. Tears began to roll faster and she started to sob.

Then the door crashed open and there stood Great Uncle Malc with his next-door neighbour, Glen, behind him.

"PACEY – SETH," he cried when he laid eyes on them, "what in the devil's name has happened…"

Just then, the other door from the tunnel burst open and the two elephant men came crashing in. The elephant men made a dash for the door, but Great Uncle Malc grabbed one of them and Glen grabbed the other. A fight broke out and the four men were knocking seven bells out of each other. One would hit the other, followed by another blow from the other. Great Uncle Malc, finally got the better of the elephant man he was fighting and tugged at his mask. The mask fell of revealing not an elephant, but an ordinary man.

"You," shouted Uncle Malc in surprise.

Great Uncle Malc stood in shock, momentarily, which gave the man enough time to hit him with his helmet. Great Uncle Malc went down like a sack of spuds.

Glen had managed to get his man in an armlock, but as he was putting him to the floor, the other assailant bashed him with the helmet he was carrying and knocked Glen out of the way. Glen was now overpowered, strong as he was, he could not take both of them on. Both villains made for Glen, when, just in the distance, the noise of a siren could be heard and blue lights were seen reflecting on the walls.

The two men looked at each other and ran out the door. Glen made a valiant attempt running after them, but they were gone.

Great Uncle Malc came to and got to his feet just as the police came through the door. "Right young lady, you have a lot of explaining to do," he said.

Her great uncle went to her and Seth and quickly ripped the duct tape off her face and hands and feet. As sore as this was, she was never so happy to be in the pain that she was in. Both children jumped up and grabbed on to their great uncle and sobbed their hearts out.

"I don't understand," sobbed Pacey, "how could you know where we were? How did you know to come?"

"That's enough for now, Pacey. I have to go with the police to sort things out. I will be a while, but I'll take you back to the house where Aunty Dot is waiting for you," said Uncle Malc, more than a little weary.

As Great Uncle Malc carried them back to the house, Great Aunty Dot and Solomon were waiting for them. Pacey was well prepared for what she had coming and was dreading it.

"You poor kids, what on earth have you been up to? What did they do to you? Are you alright? Come into the warmth and I'll heat up some hot chocolate for you. You can tell us all about it in the morning," said a very concerned Great Aunty Dot.

This was not what Pacey or Seth had expected. *Result,* thought Pacey, as she looked at her younger brother and he turned to her…winked and fell asleep.

Chapter XII
Pacey's Destiny Is Set in Stone

The morning arrived suddenly with Solomon jumping on top of Pacey's bed. "Get up, get up, lazy bones, Aunty Dot's making breakfast, eggs, bacon and tatty scones," said an excited Solomon.

Pacey sat up, rubbing her eyes, and tried to focus. Then the reality of last night hit her like a sledgehammer. POW!

She immediately fell backwards just as if she had been hit. *Oh no, I'm in so much trouble,* she thought.

Solomon was still jumping around like a mad thing. "You're in trouble, you're in trouble, you're in trouble and you owe me your life, you owe me your life," he went.

"Stop your ranting, you little weed, or I'll separate you from your breath. What do you mean I owe you my life?"

Before he could answer, Great Aunty Dot shouted up to them to get down for breakfast as it would be on the table shortly and it had better not get cold.

"You'll see," said Solomon cheekily as he ran downstairs, "you'll see."

Once at the breakfast table, Pacey looked at her great aunt and her great aunt looked at her. Not a word was said which was more upsetting as Pacey knew that what was coming was going to be a crackerjack of a scolding.

"I'm expecting your great uncle back from the police station soon," said Great Aunty Dot in a very matter-of-fact tone, "we will wait until we hear from him before we talk Pacey. Then we will have words."

Pacey's eyes started to well up and the tears began to flow.

"No need for tears, young lady, you knew you were breaking all our rules and our care for you," said her great aunt in the same matter-of-fact tone.

The time passed at an unbearable speed. Pacey looked at her watch, 8:45. In Pacey's head, two hours had passed. She looked at it again, 9:00. Time really was going slow.

By 10:00, Great Uncle Malc walked through the door, along with neighbour Glen.

"That was one heck of a night, young lady," said Great Uncle Malc as he sat down at the breakfast table.

"Sit down, sweetheart, you must be exhausted. I'll get you some breakfast and you can tell us all about it," said Great Aunty Dot.

"I'll take you through the main points and then we can decide what to do with this pair," said a weary Great Uncle Malc. "It turns out, Pacey was not the only one seeking hidden treasure. The noises and lights you saw, Pacey, were the result of two men who were trying to get to another treasure that was hidden under the tower. Yes, I said men, not elephant men. What you saw was someone wearing a welder's helmet with an air hose to take away the fumes, but you saw that anyway. When I removed the helmet from the guy I was fighting, I immediately recognised him as being Ralph, from the planning department office at the council, whom I spoke to after you said there were noises and lights coming from the tower. Once I was able to recognise him and gave his name to the police, he was easy to find. He and his accomplice are now in police custody."

Ralph, it appears, is a grandson of one of the group of men who stole the Stone of Destiny from Westminster Abbey in 1950.

The thieves worried about being captured and left the stone at the Arbroath Abbey on 11 April 1951, it was recovered and returned to Westminster Abbey, but there have always been rumours that this was a fake and that the real stone was hidden. Ralph's grandad, it turns out, also had something to do with the water tower and found out there was a possible secret tunnel at the tower. After years of searching, he found the entrance after some maintenance work was done on the tanks. He buried the stone where it now lies.

Ralph's grandad had fears that this important stone may never be recovered and brought back to its rightful place in Stirling. After all, that was the reason for stealing it in the first place to bring it back to Scotland. He told the story to Ralph on his deathbed. Ralph then recruited one of his cousins to steal it for themselves instead of returning it to the Scottish people and hold it up for ransom. It took a few years; he inveigled his way into the council planning office so he could get his hands on the plans and the keys for the tower. The problem that he faced was that the way to the tunnel was blocked by the large copper tanks inside that were used to hold water. That's why he and his cousin were welding, or more rightly, burning away large sections of the tanks until they could find the doorway to the tunnel.

"Whoa, that's great news," said Pacey excitedly, forgetting the trouble she was in, "I've saved the Stone of Destiny for the whole of Scotland!"

"Not so fast, young lady," said Great Uncle Malc, "Ralph escaped down the tunnel that Pacey had found. He didn't know that that particular tunnel existed. However, he did know that the area where the stone lay was part of the water way which used to fill the pond. The tunnel is connected to a well which was put into disuse many years ago. As he made his escape, he saw the gate connecting the well and opened it, flooding the tunnel and stopping the police from following him. So, we do not have the Stone of Destiny, it is currently under tons and tons of water. Most likely the tunnel will be in a dangerous condition for people to go into for quite some time. So, we only have Ralph's word for it, that the stone is still there. This is such an important stone of national importance; the police and the government are keeping the story quiet. They don't want other adventurers trying to find the stone and stealing it again. So, your heroism will remain unknown for quite some time, young lady."

At that, Pacey's head went down.

"But Uncle Malc, I still don't understand how you knew where to find me?" queried Pacey, delaying the inevitable punishment that was due.

"Ah well, you owe your life to young master Solomon here," as Great Uncle Malc swung around and smiled at Solomon. Solomon immediately jumped up and down smirking at Pacey and Seth. "That's enough now, Solomon. It turns out Solomon woke up and found Seth's bed empty. He went to your bedroom Pacey and once he found it empty, he knew you would be at the water tower. As there was deep snow around, your footsteps were easy to follow especially at that time of night. He arrived at the hole on the island when your head surfaced and immediately disappeared. He knew from your screams that he couldn't do anything to save you and thank goodness, had the good sense to come and get me. I went for Glen next door and the rest you have heard."

"Well, that is some story," exclaimed Great Aunty Dot as she kissed her husband on the forehead.

"On one hand; you cracked a secret code that no one has ever done and possibly saved a great piece of history being robbed and ransomed by two crooks. On the other hand, you completely disobeyed everything we told you, nearly got yourself and your brother killed, crossed a dangerous pond that you could have drowned in. You and your brothers nearly got your great uncle and Glen killed or severely injured, lost a day's work for both your great Uncle and Glen, woke up half of Arbroath with all the sirens and shouting and nearly sent me to an early grave. Just what kind of punishment do you think will suit this type of crime?"

"I'm sorry, Aunty Dot and Uncle Malc and Glen, I never thought it would end up being dangerous." Pacey sniffled.

Great Aunty Dot and Great Uncle Malc and Glen went into a huddle to discuss 'The Punishment'.

I'll never get out again, never, thought Pacey, *and it will be worse when Mum and Dad find out.*

"OK, punishment one, you will take out Roo the dog four times a day for a walk," started Great Uncle Malc.

I can live with that, thought Pacey.

"Second, you will lift and dispose of all Roo's poops during your walks and in the garden."

"Yuk."

"Third, you will not be allowed television or electronic games."

"Oooaaaahh, OK."

"Fourth."

"There's a fourth?" Pacey scowled.

"Fourth, you will do the dishes for your great aunt for every meal."

By the time of the Tenth commandment, Pacey had lost the will to live.

"Right, that will be all for now until your mum and dad get here, get Roo's lead, he needs walking, oh and don't forget the dog-poo bags."

Life as a heroine is not so glamorous, thought Pacey as she headed for the door. *I wonder what happened to the original treasure though?* and she was off.